Headwork

Book Four

Chris Culshaw

Oxford University Press
1992

Oxford University Press, Walton Street, Oxford OX2 6DP

Oxford New York Toronto
Delhi Bombay Calcutta Madras Karachi
Petaling Jaya Singapore Hong Kong Tokyo
Nairobi Dar es Salaam Cape Town
Melbourne Auckland

and associated companies in
Berlin Ibadan

Oxford is a trade mark of Oxford University Press

ISBN 0 19 833392 7

Set by Pentacor PLC, High Wycombe, Bucks
Printed in Great Britain

The illustrations are by Mike Allport p27, p28; Neil Chapman p9, p12; Derek Collard p17, p19, p21, p48, p50; Linda Jeffrey p39, p43; Colin Paine p57, p59, p60; Joanna Quinn p6; Eric Stemp p32, p35.

Cover illustration by Mike Allport

Contents

Sparks

I was in the same form as Claire Parks. I was her friend for a while, until my father heard what she got up to at school. Then he wouldn't let me go around with her. He said she was 'a bad influence'.

I'll never forget the first time I saw her. She came to our school half-way through the summer term. Our form tutor, Mrs Bates, introduced her to the class. 'This is Claire Parks. She's feeling rather nervous. This is a big school and Claire's bound to feel a little lost for a few days. So make sure you look after her, 4B.'

Nervous? A little lost? Look after her? It was soon very obvious that Claire Parks could look after herself, thank you very much.

The next day when Mrs Bates told her that she must wear a tie for school, Claire Parks said, 'I can't wear a tie Miss, I'm allergic to ties.'

Mrs Bates, twenty-five years a teacher, had never heard that one before. She said firmly, 'I want to see you in a tie tomorrow, Claire. A rule is a rule.'

'But it's true miss, honest miss. If I wear a tie I break out in spots.'

Mrs Bates smiled, a thin frosty smile. 'Claire, make sure you're properly dressed tomorrow. A rule is a rule.'

But Claire Parks believed that rules were made to be broken and the next day she came to school without a tie again. So Mrs Bates handed her the spare tie she kept in her top drawer. Her voice was like ice cracking. 'Wear this one today. Let me have it back tomorrow – when you come in your own tie.'

Claire put on the tie and went off to her first lesson. When Mrs Bates saw her at morning break her face, arms and legs were covered in large red spots. 'I told you I was allergic to ties, miss,' she said with a grin.

Mrs Bates stared at her with her ice-blue eyes. She ran a finger as cold as an icicle down Claire's cheek. 'I see you're not allergic to lipstick! Wash it off. Right now!' Her voice was straight out of Antarctica.

* * *

This was only the beginning of the battle. During the next few weeks Claire wore a tie every day. But always in a way that made blizzards blow in Mrs Bates' tidy mind.

Claire turned the tie inside out. She starched it so it stuck out from her throat like one of the blades of Boudicea's chariot wheels. Claire wore it round her waist, like a belt. Round her ankle like a snake-bite bandage. Round her wrist like a watch strap. Round her head like a freedom fighter.

Mrs Bates spat hailstones. Claire wore it under her blouse. She wore it outside her blouse, but hanging down her back, like a pigtail. She tied it in a knot that was so small you needed a magnifying glass to see it. Then a knot that was so big it hid half her face.

Claire got her sister to make her a school tie. It was four metres long and a metre wide. It billowed like a red and blue striped sail. Mrs Bates, her face a block of blue-green ice, howled, 'Enough!' Claire was buried in an avalanche of anger. She was suspended the following day.

On sports day the last event was always the Invitation Mile, a race between teachers and pupils. Mrs Bates was a very keen runner and always won this race.

The race was nearly over and she was in the lead, as usual. Suddenly, a girl, a naked girl, ran on to the track and sprinted in front of her. It was Claire Parks. She wasn't actually naked we discovered later. She was wearing a very revealing flesh-coloured body stocking, so she looked as naked as the day she was born. As she ran bare-footed towards the finishing tape I could see that she was wearing a school tie. She ran straight through the tape, down the school drive, jumped onto the back of her boyfriend's motorbike and roared away.

* * *

All this happened ten years ago. I never saw Claire Parks again after that unforgettable exit – until last night. I was watching the rock and pop awards on BBC 1. And there she was! Sara Sparks now. She was being presented with a gold disc. And very smart she was, in a suit and tie. After the presentation she sang her latest song, *Breaking all the rules*. I wondered if Mrs Bates was watching, and if Claire's song had melted her heart at last.

What to do

Oral work in pairs or small groups

1 Why do you think Claire was so determined not to wear a tie?

2 What does Mrs Bates mean when she tells Claire that 'a rule is a rule'?

3 If you had been Claire's form tutor how would you have dealt with the situation?

4 What would it be like to go to a school that had *no* rules?

5 What are the advantages of having rules? What are the disadvantages? Draw up a table, like the one below. Fill in the advantages and disadvantages that you think of.

Advantages of school rules	Disadvantages of school rules
Protects weaker students.	Can cause friction between teachers and students.

Writing

Write a story about a girl/boy who is determined not to follow a school rule about uniform, hairstyle, etc. Use the points raised in question 5 above to help you.
The boy/girl could have an argument with a teacher/parent in which points for and against rules are discussed.

The Treasure House

The Empress was the richest woman on earth. She ate from gold plates and drank from gold cups. She picked her teeth with a gold toothpick. Slaves clipped her golden toe-nails with gold scissors. She slept in a gold bed and sat upon a gold throne. Her golden palace shone so brightly in the morning sun that people passing by had to shade their eyes or be blinded.

Gold breeds gold, and before long the Empress's palace was overflowing with treasures. So she sent for Fu Lin, a master builder. She told him that he must build a treasure house for all her gold. 'It must have walls as thick as you are tall. No windows, and just one small iron door. You have a year to build it, not a day more. If you have not finished it by then . . . ' The Empress did not have to say more.

A year later the treasure house was finished and Fu Lin went to ask for his wages. The Empress gave him five small gold coins. Fu Lin said softly, 'There is no finer treasure house in all the world. It is as beautiful as the treasure that fills it. I have given you one year of my life to build it.' He looked at the coins in his work-worn hand. 'Is this all I am to get in return?'

The Empress fixed him with her small snake-like eyes. She got up from her throne and walked over to one of her guards. She drew a long gold dagger from his belt. 'So, what price do you put on the rest of your life, master builder?'

Fu Lin, bowing low, left without another word.

* * *

Fu Lin lived with his aged mother, and his younger brother Fu Hong. When he told them what the Empress had done Fu Hong said. 'Five crowns for a year's work! What a fool you've been.'

But Fu Lin smiled and said, 'Don't worry little brother, I'll get paid in full soon enough.'

About a week later Fu Lin woke his brother in the middle of the night and told him to get dressed. 'Don't make a noise, or you'll wake mother.'

'Where are we going?' whispered Fu Hong.

'You'll see. Hurry now. The moon will be up in an hour.'

* * *

The master builder led his brother through the empty streets to the back of the Empress's treasure house. Fu Hong was very frightened. 'What are we doing here, brother? If we are found here, skulking about like common criminals, she'll cut out our tongues and feed them to her goldfish.'

But his brother wasn't listening. He was running his hand along the wall of the treasure house, counting the blocks. He stopped and took a knife from his tunic. He slipped the blade between two of the huge stones and Fu Hong heard a rumble, like distant thunder. One of the stone blocks moved, revealing a secret passage into the treasure house.

Fu Lin took a candle from his tunic and lit it. 'Wait here little brother. I'll not be long.' Then he slipped head first into the passage and was gone.

A few minutes later Fu Hong heard the jingle of coins, and there was Fu Lin's candle-lit face, smiling from the secret doorway. 'Now I've been paid in full for my work,' he said and he handed Fu Hong two large sacks of gold. He closed the secret door and the brothers slipped away into the dark maze of narrow streets, just as the full moon rose over the palace.

* * *

Just as gold breeds gold, so gold breeds greed. It was so easy to steal from the treasure house that the brothers went back again, and again, and again.

It wasn't long before the Empress discovered that someone was stealing her treasure. But who? And how? It was a mystery. The Empress had put the wax seals on the iron door herself. These seals were never broken, but bags of gold still went missing.

The Empress was determined to solve the mystery. She put two iron bear-traps in the treasure house: traps with sharp jagged teeth that bit into the legs of anything foolish enough to stand on them.

On their next visit to the treasure house both brothers crawled through the secret passage as usual. It was Fu Lin who felt the trap snap tight around his foot. As he struggled to get free the second trap bit hard into his right hand.

For more than an hour Fu Hong tried to free his brother but could not. It would have taken the strength of ten to open the traps.

At last Fu Lin said, 'There is one last thing you must do for me now, little brother. You must kill me.'

Fu Hong began to sob.

'You must kill me and . . . cut off my head.'

The younger brother cried, 'No! No! There must be some other way . . . '

'There is no other way, Fu Hong. This way you and our mother will be safe. If the Empress finds out it was me that tricked her she will kill you and mother, our aunts and uncles, cousins – our whole family. She is ruthless. You know that, don't you?'

Fu Hong nodded.

'Then do it, little brother, do it!'

The next day when the Empress saw the headless body she was even more puzzled. 'So, this one had a friend. Or friends.' She still had no idea how the thieves had entered the treasure house. She ordered her guards to take the headless body and hang it on the city walls above the city gates. She offered a thousand gold pieces to anyone who could identify it.

When Fu Hong heard this he was alarmed. He made up his mind to steal the body. That night he went to the city gates pushing an old hand cart. On the cart was a large barrel of wine. Just as he got to the gate Fu Hong tipped the cart and the barrel fell to the ground with a crash. The two guards at the gate came over to see what had happened. Fu Hong looked at the cracked barrel and the wine running down the cobbled street. 'What a waste,' he said to the guards, 'I think we should drink it, don't you?'

The guards were only too happy to help Fu Hong dispose of the wine. Soon they were dead drunk and flat out on the wine-soaked cobbles. Fu Hong took his brother's body down from the hook above the city gates. He put it in the empty wine barrel and wheeled it home.

Fu Hong dug a grave for Fu Lin under the old cherry tree at the back of their house. He lay the head and body in the grave and closed the staring eyes with two heavy gold coins–coins stamped with a likeness of the Empress. 'She sees everything,' Fu Hong thought and shivered.

He went into the house and got all the gold coins he and Fu Lin had stolen from the treasure house. He scattered them over the body, then filled the grave with earth.

The next day the two guards who had helped Fu Hong drink the barrel of wine were seen hanging from hooks by the city gate. Their eyes closed with gold too.

What to do

Oral work in pairs or small groups

1 How do you know that Fu Lin expected to be cheated by the Empress?

2 Why do you think Fu Hong put the gold into Fu Lin's grave?

3 Why might Fu Hong have returned to the treasure house? What might have happened to him if he did return?

Writing

1 Retell the story as the Empress would tell it. Remember, she is a powerful and ruthless person. She felt *very* angry about the theft of gold and her inability to find the thief.

2 You are a tour guide. You take parties of tourists around the Empress's treasure house – now a ruin. As you show them round you tell them (briefly) the story of Fu Lin, Fu Hong and the gold.
Write down what you would say as you show the tourists around. It might start something like this:

> 'Ladies and gentlemen, welcome to the Empress's Treasure House. Two thousand years ago this dusty ruin was a magnificent stone building. It was built by the Empress's chief mason, Fu Lin...'

Hawk Dreaming

Midnight. An old, red Ford van pulled into the empty car park and stopped. The driver got out: a young man about twenty, dressed in a black overall. He was carrying a small rucksack. He stood by the van, listening.

Across the car park some steep stone steps led up to a large building. The building was in darkness, except for one lighted window. The security guard's office.

The young man left the van, ran silently up the steps and round to the back of the building. There was a very tall jacaranda tree close to the building. Its scented blossom looked like a cloud of purple smoke in the moonlight.

The young man climbed the tree and swung across onto the roof. He took a large screwdriver out of the rucksack and levered open a skylight.

He looked at his watch. Once inside, once his feet touched that polished floor, he would have just four minutes.

He put on the rucksack again and gripped the edge of the skylight. He swung down into the blackness, and hung there for a second or two, listening. He let go, knowing exactly where he would land, four metres below.

Thirty seconds later he was standing over a long glass case. He took out his torch, to double check. 'Not long now my brothers and sisters.'

No time to force the lock. He pulled a hammer from the rucksack and smashed the case. Before the echo of the shattering glass had died away the young man had emptied the case into his rucksack.

Two minutes later J.J. Codale, the chief security guard, ran panting into the room. He was just in time to see the young man's feet disappearing through the skylight.

When the police arrived at the museum Mr Codale wasn't able to tell them much. He'd seen the red Ford van pulling away from the car park, but he wasn't able to give a description of the driver.

'Was he alone?' asked the police sergeant.

'Couldn't be sure,' said Mr Codale, 'But one thing I am sure of – he's either dumb or crazy or both.'

'Why do you say that?'

'Well, just look around you, sergeant. This room's full of very valuable items. There's silver, ivory, coins, paintings.' He went over to one of the glass cases. 'Why, some of these pots are priceless.'

'You're right Mr Codale, it doesn't make sense, does it?'

J.J. Codale looked down at the shattered glass and the empty display case. He shook his head. 'Why did he risk breaking in here just to steal a pile of worthless, old bones?'

Because the young man had stolen 'a pile of worthless, old bones', and not the priceless Chinese pottery in the next case, the story was news. The next day the whole of Australia, from Adelaide to Darwin, saw J.J. Codale on the midday news being interviewed outside Sidney museum.

* * *

The old, red Ford van rattled through the small township of Giles. The road west out of the town into the vast Gibson Desert turned from tarmac to grit to dust. The young man was over two thousand miles from Sidney now and nearly at the end of his journey.

He should have stopped at Giles. He should have spent the night in the motel. But he didn't. He pressed on. Three days without proper sleep. He was bound to crash, and he did.

A hundred miles from Giles he fell asleep at the wheel.The old van spun off the road and plunged down a steep rocky gully. He hit his head on the windscreen and blacked out.

When he came to, hours later, he tumbled out of the van and climbed up the steep gully to the road. There was a police car parked a few metres away. The policeman had his back to him. He was on the radio, calling up a helicopter ambulance. The young man could hear snatches of conversation:

'The driver's unconscious . . .

No, I haven't moved him . . .

He's in the shade, breathing nice and easy . . .

Yes, pulse 80 . . .

Bleeding from the mouth and nose . . . Nothing serious.

I've got his licence here . . .
His name is Billy Yaramarna . . .
No, he doesn't look like an aboriginal . . .
A half-caste maybe . . .
No, he's not local . . .
He's from Sidney . . .
And guess what . . . he's driving that red Ford van.'

Billy Yaramarna didn't wait to hear any more. He scrambled back down into the shadow of the gully, pulled his rucksack from the upturned van and ran off up the dry river bed into the waiting desert. He didn't look back. The policeman would not follow him. Not on foot.

* * *

At sun-up the next day he climbed out of the river bed and looked around. It had been a cool night and not far away a frilled lizard was warming itself in the early sun.

Billy could see the red cliff, the place his grandfather called Hawk Dreaming, about ten miles to the west. Between his hiding place and the red cliff was open desert.

Billy heard the helicopter before he saw it. He dropped down between some rocks and waited. A few seconds later the helicopter came roaring up the river bed. It circled for a few minutes, then moved away east, back towards the dirt road.

The helicopter came back three times that day. It swept back and forth, over the rocky wilderness between the road and the river bed. When it flew off at sunset Billy crept out of his hiding place, and turned his face towards Hawk Dreaming.

At sun-up next day Billy stood on the top of one of the dunes and looked back the way he had come. Tell-tale footprints marked his exhausting struggle. If the helicopter came back now they would know exactly where to find him. He had to press on.

At last he stood in the shadow of the great, red cliff: Hawk Dreaming. He took out the map his grandfather had drawn for him. He must follow the cliff east, until he came to a very narrow canyon. 'This is the place,' his grandfather said, 'the sacred place, where the spirits of the dead are carried in an eagle's claws, to The Dreamtime.'

Before he entered the cool shade of the canyon Billy asked permission of the spirits, as his grandfather had told him. He had to remember everything. He had to do it right. So much depended on him.

Billy had spent hours listening to his grandfather's stories. At first they had been just that – stories. But as he got older, he began to feel the undercurrent of bitterness and anger in them. They were stories of sacred places, places of power and mystery and sadness: places like Hawk Dreaming.

Billy's mother, an aborigine like his grandfather, didn't like Billy spending so much time with the old man. She used to say, 'He's living in the past, Billy. Forget all that nonsense. It won't help you pass your exams. It won't help you get a job.'

He walked up the sandy floor of the steep-sided canyon for an hour before he found the caves. As he walked he wondered, for the first time since he broke into the museum, if he was doing the right thing. Would it work? He wasn't a full aborigine. He was a half-caste, caught between two worlds. Perhaps he was meddling in something that he wasn't really a part of. Perhaps his grandfather had been wrong.

* * *

The helicopter was overhead again. The thwack-thwack-thwack of the rotor blades filled every corner of the canyon. The rock walls seemed to vibrate. It was such a violent, alien sound it

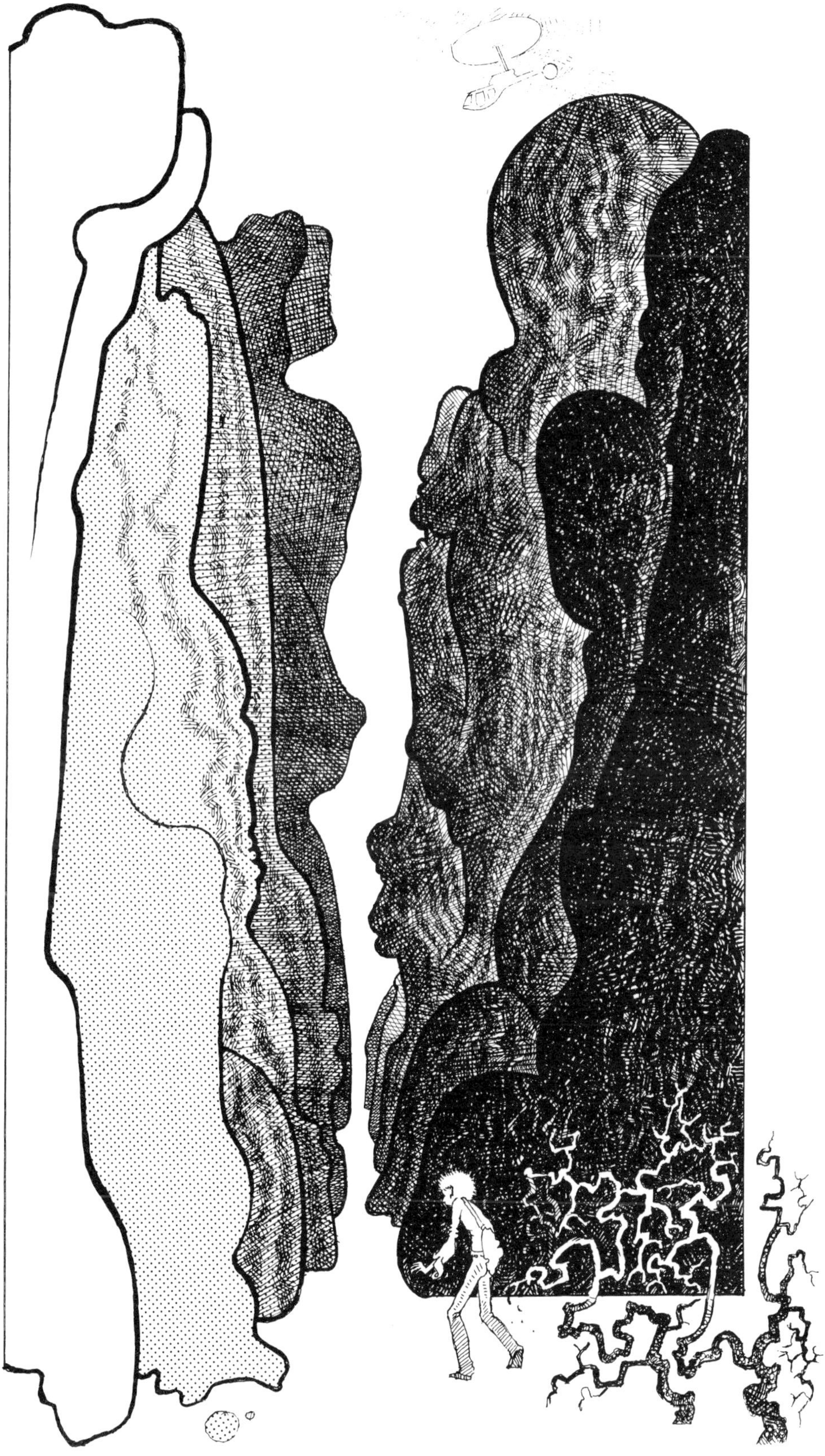

pushed all doubt from Billy's mind. Thwack-thwack-thwack. It was everything his grandfather hated. 'It will work. It doesn't matter about my skin.'

Billy knew the helicopter could never get down into the narrow canyon, so he had at least an hour's start.

He took the white powder from his rucksack and mixed it with a little water to make a thin paste. He took off his shirt and smeared the paste on his face, his chest and his arms. Then he took a mouthful of the paste, placed his hand on the rock and sprayed an outline of it next to the other ghostly hands. His grandfather's hand-print was amongst the other prints – prints that went back forty-thousand years.

All that he had to do now was put the bones in the burial cave. It was late afternoon as he started to climb. As he scrambled up the steep canyon wall the bones seemed to grow suddenly heavier. The straps of the rucksack cut into his shoulders. But Billy felt good. He remembered a time when he'd scored the winning goal in a basketball game at school. The team had carried him, head high, round the gym. He felt like that now, but this time the supporting hands were gentle, unseen.

He remembered what his grandfather had said, 'You're not doing this for yourself. It's for me, your mother, all of us. All our people, tens of thousands of us, who've been pushed out by the mining companies and the military.'

The cave was about thirty feet up. It wasn't a hard climb. Steps had been cut into the soft rock, connecting a series of wide ledges. Billy was a good climber and very soon he was on a ledge just below the entrance to the burial cave.

He took the bones from the rucksack, one by one, handling them with great care, and added them to the pile in the cave. The bones seemed warm to the touch, like living things. Billy felt a deep chill. The power, the helping hands withdrew. He was alone. But he still felt strong, in control. Suddenly, he understood the power of Hawk Dreaming.

As he was about to put the last bone in place, the skull of a small child, he saw the snake.

It snapped at Billy's hand three, maybe four times, before Billy lurched backwards and fell twenty feet to a ledge below.

He hit the ledge with a sickening smack. He heard his leg break under him. The pain in his leg boiled up into his stomach.

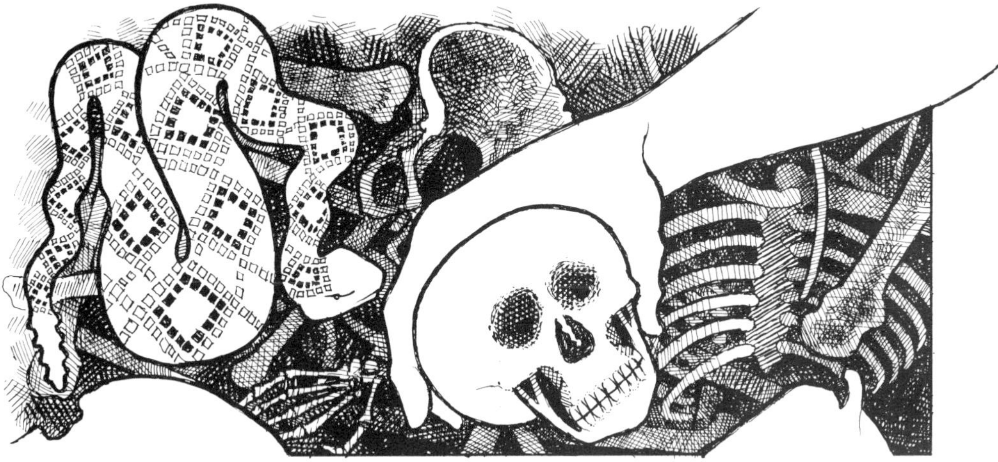

He could hear his heart thumping like a steam-hammer: each beat pumping the venom . . . Soon every cell in his body seemed to be on fire.

'The police . . . They must have found my prints by now . . . They must be near the canyon . . . ' He called out, over and over again. The gloomy canyon multiplied and magnified his voice a thousand times, as if all the spirits in The Dreamtime were crying out in sympathy. 'Help me, me, me, me . . . '

Billy Yaramarna and the spirits of Hawk Dreaming called out over and over and over . . . until they were struck dumb by the pain.

Voices.
Torch light.
The scrabble of boots on rock.
Being lifted.
Pain.
Crying out.
The spirits answering.
Carried.
Pain.
A needle in the arm.
Nothing.

Billy Yaramarna opened his eyes. There was a policeman sitting at the end of the bed, the same policeman that had found him after he'd crashed his van.

'Good day, Billy. The name's Rossi, Sergeant Rossi. Feeling better?'

'Where am I?'

'In hospital, in Alice Springs. How's the leg feel?'

Billy looked down at his leg. It was in plaster from toe to thigh. 'Feels like . . . nothing. Like it's made of stone.'

'Broken in six places. Took the doc five hours to put you together again. Lucky we had a chopper up there.' Sergeant Rossi got up and poured a glass of water. He sat down on the edge of the bed and handed Billy the glass. 'What were you doing in that canyon, Billy?'

Billy sipped the water and closed his eyes.

'You're the nut who stole the bones from the Sidney museum, aren't you?'

Billy pressed the ice-cold glass against his forehead.

'Why did you go to ground, when you crashed your van? What are you trying to hide?'

Billy Yaramarna opened his eyes. The policeman had taken out a notebook, and sat patiently, pencil in hand.

'Well Billy? You'll have to tell sooner or later. It'll all come out in court.'

Billy closed his eyes again. Court. Yes. That's where he would tell the whole story. The truth. Not the stories the tourists get to hear. The truth. How his ancestors were cheated, used, murdered. How they were treated like trash. Pushed aside by bulldozers. Made to feel like trespassers on their own land. Yes. In court. That's when he would tell the world about his grandfather, and his ancestors, and the spirits of Hawk Dreaming.

* * *

Billy Yaramarna was given a six months suspended sentence for breaking into the museum. The judge ruled that the bones were no longer 'the property of the State' and must remain at Hawk Dreaming.

After the trial Billy was surrounded by radio and TV reporters. His words were beamed by satellite across Australia. Invisible waves of energy, going out to every town and city. As Billy stood on the wide, white marble steps of Sidney Court House, telling the whole story, his words could be heard loud and clear in Hawk Dreaming, forty-thousand years away.

What to do

Oral work in pairs or small groups

1 Why did Billy say ‘Not long now my brothers and sisters’ before he broke into the glass case?

2 What was the policeman, at the scene of the crash, able to find out about Billy from his licence?

3 What do you think The Dreamtime is?

4 Why do you think Billy’s mother did not like her son spending time with his grandfather?

5 Billy felt he was ‘caught between two worlds’. What did he mean by this?

6 What do you think was ‘the power of Hawk Dreaming’?

7 Why didn’t Billy want to speak to Sergeant Rossi?

8 Why did the judge decide that the bones should stay at Hawk Dreaming?

Writing

1 You are a reporter. You have been sent to interview Billy Yaramarna about the theft of the bones and the incident in the desert.
Write a list of about ten questions that you would ask Billy. Select three or four of these questions and write the answers that Billy is likely to give.

2 After Billy appears on TV a neighbour calls at his mother’s house. This neighbour wants to know all about the incident at Hawk Dreaming. Remember, Mrs Yaramarna had wanted Billy to forget ‘all that nonsense’. She didn’t want him ‘living in the past’.
Write a conversation between Mrs Yaramarna and the neighbour. Set it out like this:

Neighbour: Have you heard from Billy yet?
Mrs Y: Yes, he's home the day after tomorrow.
Neighbour: You must be very proud of him.

Double-up Delux

Scot Melrose was a loner. He didn't have any friends – unless he had sweets, then everyone was his friend. He was in the same class as me. I didn't talk to him much but I used to see him every lunch-time in the amusement arcade by Central Pier. He used to play on the same fruit machine every day – the big Double-up Delux next to the rifle range. One day I asked him why he always played that machine, never any others. He didn't answer. He didn't even take his eyes off the whirling wheels. He just stood there, very still, the tips of his fingers dancing over the buttons.

Scot had a sister called Dawn who I really liked. I wanted to ask her to the Friday night disco on the pier. I saw her every day at school but she was always with her friends. I didn't have the nerve to ask her out, not in front of her mates. But by lunch-time on Friday I was scared she might go with someone else so I asked her, straight out. I nearly fainted when she said, 'Okay, half seven, under the clock.'

I didn't think she'd come but she did. She was waiting under the old, rusty clock when I got there just before 7.30. I didn't recognize her at first, she looked so much older with make-up and her hair up. I walked over to say hello . . . and saw Scot a few yards away, standing in the shadows. Dawn shrugged and said, 'I had to bring him. My mum wouldn't let me come otherwise.'

Scot came over and said, 'Do you want to go to the pictures?'

I looked at Dawn and said, 'I thought . . . '

'He can't dance,' she said.

'I don't want to dance with him,' I said, 'I want to dance with you.'

'I'll pay,' said Scot. 'I've got loads of money.'

'Oh . . . all right,' I said.

Scot paid for us all – the best seats – and bought us sweets and ice-cream. On the way home we had fish and chips and a can of coke. I asked him how much pocket money he got.

'He wins it,' Dawn said, 'on the slot machines.'

Scot got quite mad with his sister for saying this. He snatched the can of coke she was drinking and threw it across the street saying, 'You promised, you promised.' Then he walked off home by himself.

* * *

I saw Dawn again that Sunday in the park. I asked her about Scot and the money but she wouldn't talk about it.

I didn't see Scot until Monday morning at school. He was sitting behind the bike sheds with a bag of sweets. He held out the bag and I sat down beside him. 'Our Dawn likes you,' he said without looking at me.

'Where do you get all your cash, Scot? From the slots?' I said.

He didn't answer.

'But you can never win on those machines. My mum says it's a mug's game. You have to spend twenty pence to win ten.'

Still no answer.

Just then the bell went for the end of break. Scot stood up and dropped the bag of sweets into my lap. He walked away without saying a word.

That night after school I walked home with Dawn as far as the end of her street. We sat on the wall by the chip shop. I took the bag of sweets out of my school bag and offered her one. I said, 'Your brother gave me these.'

'Scot likes you. He doesn't have any real friends. My mum worries about him. She says he . . . '

'Can you come out tonight?' I said, changing the subject.

'I'm not sure.'

'Seven o'clock, by the pier?'

'I'll try.'

* * *

I missed the bus that night, so I didn't get to the pier until quarter past seven. There was no sign of Dawn . . . but Scot was there. He smiled at me as I walked over to the clock. I'd never seen him smile before. It was a weird smile, like a clown's. He said, 'Dawn couldn't come. She had to take my dad's overalls to the laundrette. So I came instead.'

'What's up with you, Scot? Are you queer or something? I had a date with your sister . . . not you!'

He turned away, as if I'd slapped him and walked off along the pier towards the amusement arcade. I stood there for a while, under the rusty old clock, wondering what to do. If I had known what was going to happen next I would have got on the next bus home. But I didn't. For some reason, I don't know why, I followed Scot down the pier and into the arcade.

He was standing in front of the Double-up Delux. I went over and stood next to him. He tapped the pockets of his parka and I heard the clink of coins. 'I've got nearly twenty quid on me,' he said.

'How much?' I said, in disbelief.

'I can't lose.'

'Don't be . . . '

'You don't believe me, do you? You think I've nicked it, don't you?'

'Yeh . . . I don't know . . . maybe.'

He pushed some money into my hand, a fistful of 10p's. 'Go on,' he said with that silly clown's smile, 'you try.'

I pushed 10p into the slot on the big Double-up Delux and the machine burst into life. The reels were a whirling grey blur. Minutes before they stopped Scot turned to me and whispered, 'This time you lose.'

He was right. The reels showed two apples and a pear – no pay out.

I tried again. Once again, while the reels were still whirling Scot said, 'This time you lose,' and he was right again. I tried over and over to win on that machine, but couldn't. And each time Scot knew that I would lose.

'It must be fixed. My mum says they fix the reels so you can't win.' I said. Scot stepped up to the machine, dropped a coin in the slot and said very quietly, 'Watch.'

The reels began to spin, and as they were spinning, very fast, Scot turned to me and said softly, 'Three cherries.'

When the reels stopped a few seconds later they showed three bright red cherries and the machine belched out 60p.

Scot put another coin in the slot and said, 'This time . . . three melons.'

WIN!

When the three melons rolled slowly into view and the machine paid out two pounds Scot said, 'Now do you believe me?'

He played the Double-up Delux machine eleven times and won every time. And every time he told me what he would win and how he would win it, long before the reels had stopped.

Then without warning Scot walked out of the arcade onto the pier. I ran after him and grabbed his arm, 'Hang on Scot. Why don't you clean it out? You're daft. There must be a few hundred quid in that machine!'

He didn't answer. He wandered off towards the little café near the end of the pier. He shouted over his shoulder, 'Come on, I'll buy you a hot-dog.'

As we were leaving the café with our hot-dogs we bumped into a kid pushing through the narrow doorway. I recognized him straight away. He was a punk, about seventeen years old. He used to go to our school, until he'd been thrown out. I had dropped my hot-dog and when I bent down to pick it up the punk slammed his boot down on my hand. The hot-dog was squashed flat and ketchup oozed out between my fingers. I cried out in pain. The punk laughed and said, 'Naughty, naughty! Didn't they teach you about germs at that school? Can't eat that now, can we?'

He took his foot off my hand and grabbed me by the hair, 'Empty your pockets, Cry-baby!'

'I haven't got any money, honest,' I said trying to fight back the tears.

Without warning he let go of me and turned to Scot, 'But *you* have, haven't you? I've seen you playing that Double-up Delux. Come on, where is it?'

But Scot was off like a greyhound, past the café, off into the darkness, towards the far end of the pier. As he ran I could hear the jingle of coins as they fell from his pockets on to the wooden planking of the pier.

'Proper little moneybags, isn't he, your mate?' sneered the punk. And he started to follow Scot, slowly, hands in pockets, whistling. He knew Scot was trapped, and so did I.

* * *

'You ran way and left him, didn't you! And he thought you were his mate.' That was all Dawn said to me after the inquest. She never spoke to me again, never.

It was in all the papers. Scot's body was pulled out of the sea the next day. The police said he had drowned because of the weight of the money in his parka pockets.

I had to go to court, as a witness. When it was my turn to answer questions I was shaking like a leaf. One of the magistrates asked me why I had left Scot on his own, why had I run away. I couldn't answer. I just stood there, crying and crying, as the questions whirled round like the reels on the big Double-up Delux. Round and round they whirled, whispering, 'This time you lose . . . this time you lose . . . '

What to do

Oral work in pairs or small groups

1 What kind of person was the story-teller? What can you deduce from the story about his character, his attitudes, etc?

2 What kind of person was Scot?

3 What makes a person 'a loner'?

4 How did the story-teller feel when Scot came along with Dawn on that first date?

5 How do you think Dawn felt about this situation?

6 When the story-teller asked Dawn about the money (in the park) why wouldn't she talk about it?

7 When Scot came to the pier by himself (instead of Dawn) the story-teller didn't go home, but followed Scot into the arcade. Why do you think he did this?

8 If Scot could win any time he wanted, why do you think he didn't empty the machine?

Writing

1 After Scot's death the story-teller was tormented by guilt. He blamed himself for Scot's death. For months afterwards he had terrible nightmares.
Describe one of these dreams in about eight to ten sentences. Try to use images or phrases from the story.
Remember, in dreams the real world often becomes distorted and disturbing.
e.g. The Double-up Delux machine might seem to be 50 metres tall. It might have pictures of Scot's parents on the reels, instead of fruit.

2 If Scot hadn't run off the wrong way – down the pier, to a dead end – the story may have had a very different ending. Write an alternative ending for the story, starting with the line:
'I haven't got any money, honest,' I said.

3 You are the police officer called to the pier the night Scot is drowned. Write a report of the incident. This should include:
A The time and place the body was found.
B A description of the clothing, items in pockets, etc.
C Who identified the body.
D Who you interviewed and what they said.
You will need to include times, dates, names, etc. Some of these will come from the story, others will have to be invented.

Flesh and Blood

Jill Duggan's mother fell in the barn six weeks before Christmas and broke both her wrists. 'Damn and blast!' she said angrily as Jill drove her home from the hospital. 'Six weeks in plaster! How could I have been so stupid? Just when we're coming up to our busiest time. What are we going to do, Jill? All those turkeys . . .'

'Don't worry, mum. We'll cope.'

'Maybe your dad could help out.'

'No, mum. We've managed without him for two years. All he ever did was spend any money we had on drink. We'll manage mum.'

'Perhaps I should ring him up and . . . '

'Mum, if he comes back then I go.'

'But . . . '

'No buts, mum. I mean it.'

They drove the rest of the way home in silence.

Joyce Duggan and her eighteen-year-old daughter Jill owned a small farm in the Yorkshire Dales. In the summer they made a good living taking visitors pony trekking across the moors. They had fifteen ponies at the farm as well as a few sheep and cows.

They also made money by fattening up turkeys. They bought one-month-old turkey chicks in September and kept them in the field with the shed behind the stables. This year they had about fifty turkeys and hoped to sell them all in the weeks before Christmas.

Three days after Mrs Duggan broke her wrists Jill came running into the kitchen. 'Mum, something's been at the birds!'

'Oh no! How many have we lost?'

'I'm not sure. There's feathers half-way up the lane behind the stable. Was it a fox do you think?'

'Must be, Jill. Nothing else would take a fully grown turkey. Nothing on four legs anyway.'

'What do you mean? Poachers?'

'Could be. The landlord of the Royal Oak said that three farms up the valley have lost birds this year.'

'Should we 'phone the police then?'

'Not much they can do, Jill. No. Go and get the gun. I'll sit up tonight.'

'Don't be daft, mum. You can hardly hold the gun, let alone shoot with it. I'll sit up.'

After tea Jill went to get the gun from under her mother's bed. It was a single barrel shot gun. It had belonged to her father. When he had moved out, two years ago, he gave it to her mother, saying, 'More use to you now, Joyce. I won't get much chance to shoot rabbits driving a milk tanker.'

As Jill sat in the kitchen cleaning the gun she tried not to think about her father. But he crept into her thoughts, like a fox. Jill tried to remember the good times when she was a child. But she couldn't hold those memories for long.

Within minutes it all came flooding back. Waking to hear shouts, sometimes screams, in the dead of night. The name-calling at school. Never having decent clothes. Never having a holiday. And her mother – always so tired. Wanting to help her, but not knowing how. In the end retreating into silence, like an animal hibernating.

Her parents finally got divorced, but none of their neighbours knew the truth. Most of them felt sorry for her father. Once Jill had overheard someone talking about him in the pub. 'Oh yes, heart of gold, Tom Duggan. Always ready to buy a round. Good laugh too. Never a dull moment when Tom's around. Drinks a bit too much now and then, but who doesn't!'

Jill loaded the gun, filled a flask with hot tea and pulled on her wellingtons. She put on her woollen hat, scarf and gloves. Then she remembered what her father used to tell her, 'Gloves and guns don't mix,' and she stuffed her gloves into her coat pocket. She said goodnight to her mother and went out to the barn.

From the back of the barn, high up in the bales of hay, she had a clear view of the lane behind the turkey field. She made a comfortable nest in the hay and settled down to wait.

Nothing. After three nights Jill was getting fed up. Then one afternoon she met Betty the Egg Woman outside the post office. 'You caught that fox yet, Jill?'

'No, Betty. There's been no sign of it since it took the turkey.'

'My first husband knew all about foxes. He was a gamekeeper. He used to say "foxes wear watches" – they'd always come at the same time. Funny that, isn't it?'

'How did he catch them? With traps?'

'No, he used eggs.'

'Eggs?'

'He used to get pheasants' eggs and inject rat poison into them. They're very fond of eggs are foxes.'

'If we tried that out stupid dogs would eat them! They're all as daft as ninepence.'

Betty climbed into her old green van and was about to drive off when she said, 'Have you tried polystyrene?'

Jill shook her head.

'Rub polystyrene on glass – one of those ceiling tiles will do the trick. It makes a noise like an injured rabbit. They say that a fox can hear it two miles away on a still night.'

Jill smiled. 'Thanks, Betty. I'll try it tonight.'

Betty started up the van. 'I saw your dad yesterday, Jill. You and him still not speaking?'

Jill bit her lip. 'There's nothing to say.'

'He was looking a bit lost. It's no fun being on your own, especially at Christmas.' With that she crashed her van into gear and drove off.

Jill, hurt and angry, walked back up the hill to the farm.

* * *

For the next three nights Jill sat up in the barn again. From time to time she rubbed the broken ceiling tile on the glass. The noise went right through her. 'Yes,' she thought, 'it sounds just like an animal in pain.' But the fox did not return.

Jill needed sleep. It was very near Christmas now. The turkeys would have to be killed and plucked soon. Her mother wouldn't be able to help much, so Jill stopped sitting up all night. She checked the turkeys before she went to bed, and got up at about four o'clock to check again.

Two nights passed and the fox was back. More feathers in the lane behind the stables. Jill was very angry. Each bird was worth more than five pounds now.

Joyce Duggan was feeling guilty because she hadn't been able to help Jill catch the fox. One morning over breakfast she said to Jill, 'I think I know a way to catch that fox. Something I read about in a magazine. I ripped the page out. Here it is.'

It was an advert for security lamps – special lights that switch themselves on when someone comes near them. 'They detect an intruder's body heat,' Mrs Duggan said. 'If it'll catch vermin on two legs, it'll catch a fox too. It's worth a try, Jill.'

Two days later they bought a security lamp and fixed it to a gate post near where they had discovered the feathers. It was connected to a couple of tractor batteries in the barn.

Jill tested it. It worked perfectly. As soon as she was within range of the lamp it lit up the whole lane, like bright sunlight.

Jill woke with a start at about three the next morning. The light was on! She picked up the shot gun and very slowly looked over the top of the bales behind which she had been sleeping.

There, in the lane, just a few metres away, was a man. He was crouching, like an animal cornered, crouching on all fours. Jill

called out, 'I've got a gun. Don't move.' He stood up, slowly, like someone waking from a long sleep. The brilliant light was right behind him, so his face was in deep shadow. Jill shouted, 'Don't move or I'll shoot!' The shadow swayed and lurched towards the barn. Jill felt her whole body tighten like a spring. Her hand on the barrel, her finger on the trigger, both felt dead, metallic. They were part of the weapon, no longer her flesh and blood. Her brain said, 'Shoot.' But the finger on the trigger would not move.

The man was very close now. She willed the dead finger back to life. Metal turned to flesh and blood. As she pulled the trigger she heard her mother call out, 'Jill! Don't! It's Tom! It's your father!'

* * *

Tom Duggan was a very lucky man. He'd been drinking heavily that night. He'd passed out, drunk, and fallen flat on his face just as Jill fired the gun.

Later, when Jill and her parents were sitting round the kitchen table drinking tea, Tom tried to laugh it off. 'If our Jilly wasn't such a bad shot I'd be dead drunk.'

Joyce Duggan looked at him and shook her head gently as if to say, 'Not now, Tom. Not now.'

Jill hadn't spoken since they helped her father in from the lane. She was trembling so much that she couldn't drink her tea without slopping it on the table. She looked across at her father. His hands were shaking too. Jill got up from the table, went over to her mother, kissed her and went upstairs to bed.

Joyce came into Jill's room just as dawn was breaking over the hill behind the farm. She said, 'He's gone. He had a bath and I gave him some breakfast. He wanted to stay, to speak to you. But I didn't think you would want him to.'

Jill pulled the duvet around her shoulders and sat up in bed. 'Why has he been stealing our turkeys?'

'He hasn't.'

'Then . . . what was he doing in the lane last night?'

'Just looking.'

'Looking! You mean he's been hanging about the farm, skulking about like a peeping tom? Watching us?'

'No, Jill. No, he meant no harm. He wanted so much to see you. He told me last night that he's been coming to the farm for weeks, late at night.'

'And just standing in the lane, watching the house?'

'Yes, Jill.'

Jill Duggan slipped back down under the duvet, turned over and buried her face in the pillow.

Her mother sat on the bed for a long time. Then she said suddenly, 'I said he could come for Christmas dinner. Is that all right?'

Jill said, very softly, 'Yes' and slipped away into a deep, deep sleep.

* * *

On New Year's Day Jill opened the kitchen door and found a dead fox lying on the doorstep. It had been shot in the head. There was a note pinned to it:

'Jilly, this is the fox that was taking your birds. I'm shooting a bit straighter these days – given up drinking. Have you made any resolutions this year? Dad.'

Jill picked up the fox and carried it towards the barn. Under the blooded fur she could feel the animal's flesh and bones, and the last embers of its body heat. By the time she had reached the barn she knew what her New Year's resolution would be.

What to do

Oral work in pairs or small groups

1 How did Jill feel about her father?

2 How did Jill's mother feel about her father?

3 Why was Jill angry after she had spoken to Betty?

4 Do you think Jill wanted her mother and father to get back together again?

5 Why did Tom Duggan come to the farm late at night?

6 How do you think he felt when he was discovered there by his daughter?

7 What was it that saved his life that night?

8 What do you think Jill's New Year's resolution would be?

Writing

1 Jill has a close friend who lives abroad. Jill writes to this friend very often.
The day after Tom Duggan's late night visit to the farm Jill wrote to her friend. The letter began:

> Dear Jo,
> Thanks for your last letter. It was good to hear all your news.
> You'll never guess what happened last night...

Finish the letter. Remember to write about Jill's feelings, as well as including details about the fox, the turkeys, the lights and the gun.

2 Jill's mother has decided to have Tom back. Jill is still uncertain.
Write a dialogue between Jill and Joyce Duggan. Mrs Duggan is trying to persuade Jill it would be worth a try.
It might begin something like this:

Joyce: I think he deserves one more chance.
Jill: I'm not sure, mum. We seemed to be getting on so well without him.

Remember, try to put both points of view across. Try also to use the incidents from the story, eg. Jill might argue that Tom's late night visits show that he is odd or disturbed. Joyce might argue that they show he cares deeply about his daughter.

The Real Thing

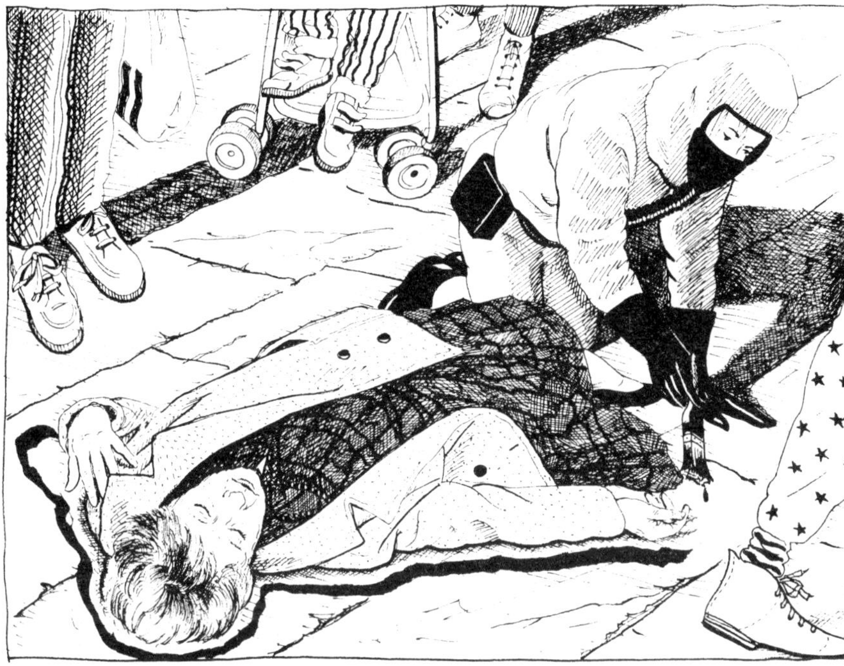

I nearly fell over her. She was face down on the cold, wet tarmac: an old woman in a green coat. I looked round for my mother. She was talking to someone outside the bread shop on the other side of the square. I shouted, but she didn't hear me.

The square was busy, but no one seemed to want to stop and help. I knelt down beside the woman and tried to remember what I'd learned at school about first aid. 'A for airways. B for breathing. C for . . . what?'

I turned her head to one side and put my ear to her mouth. She was breathing. I pinched her cheek gently and said, 'Can you hear me? Are you all right?'

She smiled and said, 'No. I'm dead.' Then she turned over and lay on her back with her eyes closed.

'Stand back! Stand back there. Let the Body Squad through!

Stand back, please.' Suddenly, I was pushed aside by two people in white boiler suits. They were each wearing red rubber boots and gloves and masks that covered most of their face.

By now a small group of people had gathered round the old woman on the ground. They pressed forward to see what was going on.

Then three more white-suited figures appeared. One, a woman, was carrying a tin of paint. She bent down and painted a bright red outline around the old woman on the ground. She stood up and shouted, 'Okay. Tag it and get rid of it!' Then she moved off quickly across the square.

My mother came over from the shops and stood by me. 'What's happened, Jon?'

I said, 'I thought she'd fainted or something but . . . '

'Stand back! Keep well back! Let the stretcher crew through!' Two more white figures joined the others.

A long red label was pinned to the old woman's green coat. Then she was lifted onto a stretcher and covered with a stiff white plastic sheet. On the sheet, in large red letters, it said: 'Danger. Contaminated corpse.'

* * *

It was nearly two o'clock that afternoon before mum and I got home. Paul, my elder brother, was in the kitchen polishing his army boots. He was in a bad mood. He was going away, camping with the local army cadets, and mum had promised to run him down to the bus station.

Mum said, 'I'm sorry, Paul. Traffic in town was murder. Couldn't get through by the town hall. Had to go all round by the park. That daft lot from the university! Protesting again. Lying in the road this time, stopping the traffic!'

'They were giving out leaflets,' I said to my brother, 'about nerve gas and germ warfare. I got one for you.' I gave it to Paul, but he threw it down on the table without even looking at it. He stuffed his boots into his kit bag and zipped it up. 'Come on, mum! If I'm late I'll be spud bashing for the rest of the week.'

I went out to the front gate to wave goodbye. I was glad Paul was going off to camp. It was the school half-term. I would have the bedroom we shared all to myself for a week. And I'd be able to use his stereo.

When my mother came back I made her a cup of tea and we sat by the fire. I said, 'It's nice, having the house to ourselves, isn't it mum?'

'Oh, did I forget to tell you, Jon? Your grandad's coming to stay for a few days. He can have Paul's bed. You don't mind do you? Sharing, I mean?'

'No, mum.'

'Sure?'

'Sure.' I couldn't hide my disappointment, not like an adult. I gave myself away too easily. It was as if my voice suddenly belonged to someone else. 'It's okay, honest mum,' said this stranger, 'I like grandad.'

It wasn't too bad, sharing the bedroom with grandad. He liked to go to bed early and he was always asleep by the time I tip-toed in. He snored and talked in his sleep. But then, Paul was forever telling me I did that too.

On Friday grandad asked me to take him down to the library. 'Let's get out from under your mother's feet, eh?'

As we walked across the market square my grandfather stopped and pointed with his stick. 'What's all this then?'

The red painted outlines. Bodies – about a dozen of them. They had been worn quite faint already. Most of them were just vague blurs, like out of focus photographs. Some children were hopping on and off them like stepping stones.

But the outline of the old woman in the green coat near the library steps was still quite sharp.

'They were protesting about nerve gas, grandad. "Long haired layabouts" mum calls them. They were dying all over town, last Saturday. It looked real. People in white coats came and took them away. They were giving out leaflets. I got one for our Paul.'

Grandad poked at the red outline of the old woman. 'Leaflets? What about?'

'Nerve gas. Germs. Chemical weapons, all that sort of stuff.'

He traced the outline of the body with his walking stick and stood staring down at it for a long time. Then he slipped his arm through mine and we shuffled up the wide stone steps into the library.

* * *

I woke with a start when my bedside light came on. Grandad was standing by my bed, holding his pyjama bottoms. I looked at my watch. It was half past two in the morning. 'Grandad, it's the middle of the night. What . . . '

'I've wet myself, Sarge, peed in my bunk.' He held out the pyjamas.

'Grandad, you're dreaming. You're not in the war. This is *our* house. This is *me*, Jonathan.'

He looked at me, blinking, then at the pyjamas. 'Making more work for your mother. She'll not be pleased . . . ' He started to shiver.

I slipped out of my bed. 'Come on. You get in here grandad, I'll fix Paul's bed. You go to sleep. There's clean sheets in the airing cupboard. Mum's not to know.'

I took his wet pyjamas and helped him into bed. I covered him with my duvet, and switched off my bedside light.

When I was changing the sheets on Paul's bed I found grandad's glasses under the pillow, and the leaflet about nerve gas. Why had he been reading that I wondered.

By the time I climbed into Paul's bed my grandfather was asleep. I couldn't sleep and lay awake listening to his irregular breathing.

After a while he began to talk in his sleep. I tried to make sense of what he said, like a detective piecing together clues.

'It's Sid! . . .'

'He's in the wire, sarge! . . . '

'Stretcher bearers! . . . '

'Sid . . . I'll get you.'

'Don't leave him there . . . '

'We can't leave him there . . . '

'Sid! . . . '

* * *

The next day, Saturday, grandad was up before mum and me. He'd washed the sheets and pyjamas and hung them out to dry. He'd made the breakfast and was sitting by the fire reading the paper when I came downstairs. 'Shall I take your mother breakfast in bed? Will she fancy an egg?' He bustled around getting a tray ready and I took it upstairs.

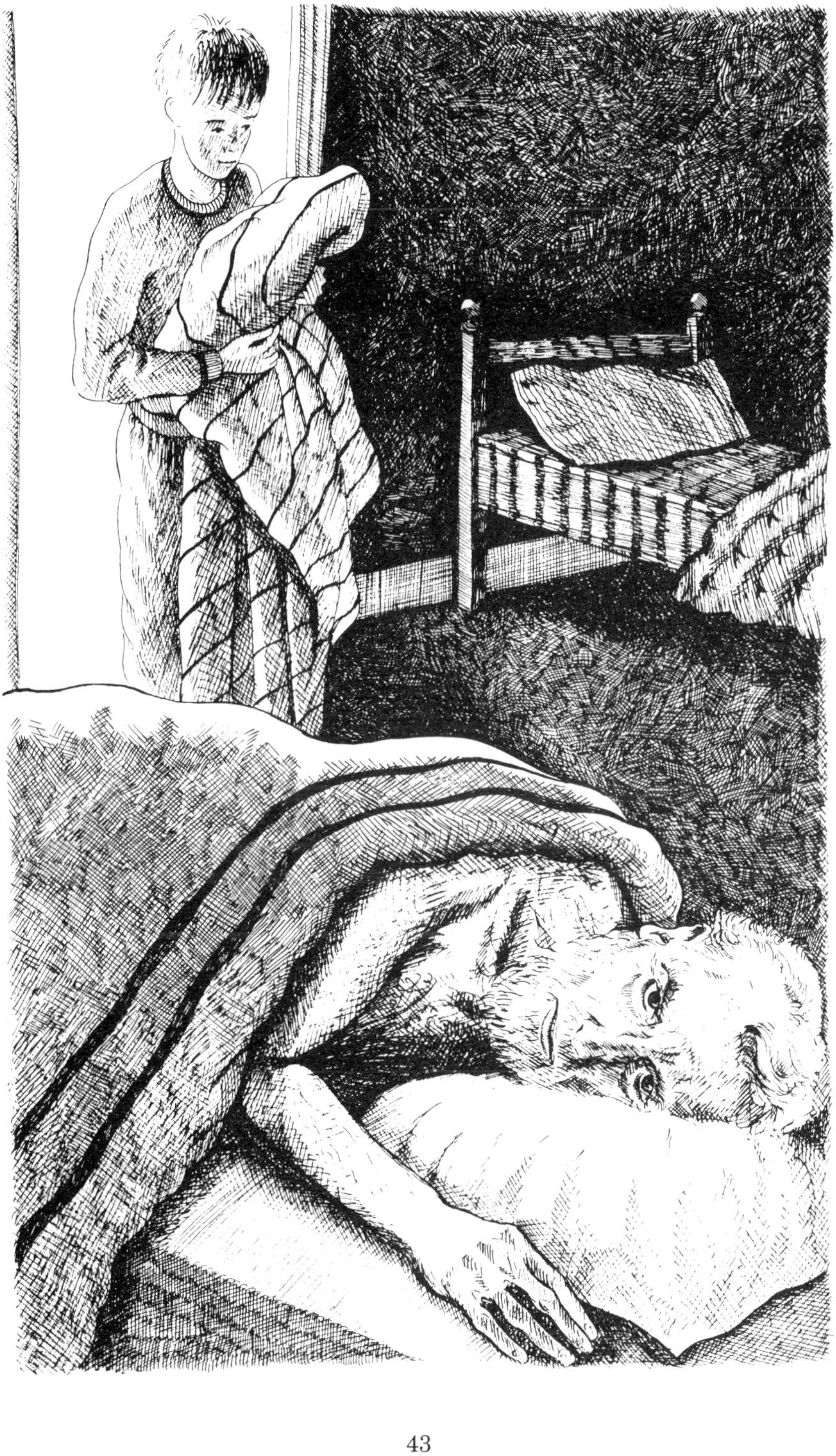

After breakfast I helped him clear away and wash up. Then we had our usual game of cards.

Mum stayed in bed until mid-day, getting up just before Paul came back from camp. He was still in his uniform, and he had black smudges on his face, like war-paint. Mum kissed him, getting black on her face too. 'What have you been up to? Haven't they heard of soap and water in the army?'

'It's face paint, mum – camouflage. We've been on night exercises. With proper weapons and live ammo. The sergeant said it was just like the real thing.'

Later that day I took grandad back to his flat in a taxi. I carried his case up to the door and he said, 'Come in and have a cup of tea. I've got some of those chocolate biscuits you like.'

When we were sitting by the gas fire drinking our tea I asked the question that had been running through my head all day, 'Grandad, who's Sid?'

It must have been almost a minute before he answered. 'He was . . . a friend. A young soldier. Not much older than our Paul.'

'He got tangled up in wire, didn't he? You were talking about him last night, in your sleep. Did he get medals, like you, grandad?'

He looked past me, as if he was talking to someone else. 'No, you didn't get a medal if you died of hunger.'

'Hunger? What do you mean, grandad?'

'I mean my best friend, Sid – Corporal Sidney George Coyle – starved to death. He got gum rot. All his teeth started to fall out. We were having to eat mouldy spuds and when they'd gone we ate the peelings. Sid couldn't chew potato peelings. He got sick and was as weak as a baby. He just gave up the ghost. He just curled up in his blanket and died. You didn't get a medal for that, Jon.'

I said, 'Why didn't somebody . . . '

'Time you were getting back home, Jonathan,' he said and pressed a pound coin into my hand. 'Here's a medal for looking after a silly old man. You know . . . last night. You're a good lad. There's a lot of your mother in you.'

I stopped at a newsagents to buy some sweets. As I sat on the wall by the bus stop I thought about what my grandfather had told me. He'd never spoken about the war before, not to me or my brother. Paul, who was 'army mad', always wanted to see his medals. He kept them in a kitchen drawer. Hidden away, under a jumble of letters, and string and crumpled bingo cards.

As I crunched my mint imperials I couldn't help thinking about my grandfather's friend, Corporal Coyle. And his bleeding gums. What, I wondered, had prompted my grandad to tell me about him? The leaflet?

When I got home I went straight up to the bedroom and slipped what was left of the mints under Paul's pillow, beside the leaflet.

What to do

Oral work in pairs or small groups

1 What do you think the story-teller, Jonathan, felt when he saw the bodies in the market square?

2 How did his mother react?

3 What was the point of the protest?

4 Why did Jonathan give the leaflet to his brother Paul?

5 What do you think the grandfather thought when he saw the outlines of the bodies in the market square?

6 Why do you think the grandfather never talked about the war?

7 How do you think Paul would have reacted if his grandfather had told him about Corporal Sidney Coyle?

8 Do you think Paul read the leaflet?

Role-play in pairs or small groups

Paul's mother called the protesters in white suits 'that daft lot from the university'. She was angry because their protest had caused a traffic jam.

Some protesters, like the anti-war protesters in the story, believe that the only way to get their message across is to break the law.

Role-play a conversation between one of the white-suited protesters and someone who thinks such actions are wrong.

Writing

When the grandfather died he left his medals to Paul. With them was a letter. The letter began:

> Dear Paul,
> I am leaving you these medals because I know you always wanted them. I don't want you to think I was brave, because they pinned these on my tunic. Thousands of really brave men died without medals. So these belong to them too.
> I know you've set your heart on being a soldier. But...

Complete the letter.
Does the letter try to persuade Paul *not* to join the army? Or does the grandfather think Paul is doing the right thing?
The story gives you some clues about how the grandfather feels about war. Try to use these in the letter to Paul.

Bristers and Sothers

I discovered Pauline Lesley North by accident. I had asked my computer for the life-scan of Lesley Pauline North, the actress, and it came up with P. L. North by mistake. I was just about to press the 'dump' button, to clear the screen and start again, when I noticed something very interesting about Pauline Lesley North – her date of birth: 29 July 2129.

I rang the editor's office right away and said, 'Can I drop that story you wanted me to write on Lesley North, the movie star? I'm on to something else much more interesting.'

The answer was short and sweet. No. If I wanted to go chasing rainbows I had to do it in my own time.

I said, 'But I think . . . '

'You're a trainee reporter. You're not paid to think, Ms Hayman. You're paid to write about video stars. We want that story on Lesley North by noon tomorrow.'

It took me six weeks to fix up an interview with Pauline North. She didn't have a vision-phone and she didn't answer my fax-flash. I spent each Monday (my day off) for a month watching her flat but she never seemed to go out. She had only one visitor, a small man with dark, deep-set eyes. He called every Monday at the same time and stayed for about an hour.

One Monday I followed this man when he left Pauline North's flat. He walked across town for about a mile. He didn't use the electric pavement. It was as if he was scared of them. I followed him to the North End, past the clone farms and the reservoir, heavily guarded by the army now, since the Water War. The slogans were still visible on the bullet-marked walls: 'Water for all', and 'If we can't have it nobody will'. I'd done two or three stories on the Water War. I still had nightmares about it. All those funerals. The tiny coffins, row on row. How could anyone poison thousands of children? What had they achieved?

I paused for a moment by the reservoir but moved on when a guard on the wall turned his binoculars on me. I'd lost sight of

is THis what they died for?
THE GENERALS ARE CLOWNS
FREE WATER NOW

the man. I hurried on towards the School Tower, and saw him go into a small bar nearby. There was always trouble with rats in this part of town. They'd attacked three children from the School last week. I felt very uneasy as I followed the man into the dimly-lit bar.

The man was sitting on his own, in the corner. I bought a drink and sat down next to him. 'You know Pauline North, don't you?'

He gave me a long hard stare. His mouth began to twitch. He put his hand to his face. 'Are you . . . the police?' he asked, looking over my shoulder.

'No,' I said. 'I'm a reporter with the Video News. The name's Suzi Hayman.'

We shook hands but he didn't tell me his name. He wouldn't let me tape our conversation. He wouldn't talk about himself. He wasn't very keen to talk about Pauline North either. He did tell me that he went shopping for her, every Monday – a few groceries, water. Nothing much.

'Are you a relative?'

'No.'

'A friend?'

'No. Not really. She helps me . . . and I do small favours for her in return.'

'She helps you, in what way?'

He looked nervously round the bar. 'She's a teacher. I go for lessons.'

'What kind of lessons?'

He fixed me with his dark, sad eyes for a long minute and looked slowly round the half empty bar again before he answered. 'History. Mrs North gives me History lessons.'

Now it was my turn to look over my shoulder.

The sad-eyed man was called Peter Jones. I met him again a few weeks later. He told me that he had persuaded Pauline North to meet with me. I went to her flat the next day, after dark.

* * *

She was much taller than I expected, and her hair was still strong and dark. 'Come in,' she said, and she showed me into a room lined with books. Hundreds of books. Real books.

I'd seen a few pictures of books, and holograms of them. Being so close to so many real ones made me feel uneasy.

We sat down by the fire. I took out my recorder, switched it on and set it down on the carpet between us. Pauline North smiled, and pointing to the recorder said, 'Does it tell the truth, Ms Hayman, that little machine of yours?'

'I'm sorry,' I said, not understanding her question.

'Never mind. My little joke. Now, why on earth do you want to interview me?'

'Are you really one hundred and twenty-six years old, Miss North?'

'Yes. I was born on 29th July in 2129, in Bristol Infirmary.'

'So you had a mother?'

'Yes, she was one of the last.'

'You were made . . . inside her?'

She looked at me with her very pale blue eyes as if that question had cut a little too deep. 'Why do you really want to interview me, Ms Hayman?'

'Why Miss North, you're the oldest person in this zone, in the whole country maybe. Our viewers will want to know all about you, what you've seen and done, what sort of life you've lived . . . '

'A very ordinary life, I assure you.'

'But you were born in the old way. You had a mother *and* a father. You're probably the only person alive today who can say that.'

She frowned. 'You make me sound like some kind of freak, Ms Hayman. A fossil.'

'I'm sorry Pauline – may I call you Pauline? I didn't mean to be rude.'

'It was normal then, you know. People thought nothing of it. There was no other way.'

'Did you have any . . . what were they called . . . bristers or sothers?'

Pauline laughed out loud. 'You mean sisters and brothers? Yes, I had two sisters and a brother. All dead.'

'And did your mother . . . make those too, in the old way?'

'She did, with a little help from my father. I would have had more bristers and sothers, as you call them, but the law was changed and my mother didn't want to risk being sent to prison.'

'Prison? What was that?'

'A sort of punishment.'

'Like the Brain Laser?'

'No, no . . . not at all like the Brain Laser. If you broke the law in those days they locked you away and then . . . forgot about you. That was prison, Ms Hayman.'

'How cruel.'

'You're taking quite a risk coming here, Ms Hayman. You know that don't you?'

'Yes . . . yes. Peter Jones told me about his lessons.'

'Were you followed?'

'I don't think so.'

'Does anyone from your office know you are here?'

'No.'

I got up and walked over to the bookshelves. 'Are they *all* History books?'

'Yes.'

'So many?'

The old woman laughed. 'The Earth is four thousand six hundred million years old, Suzi.'

No one at my school had been allowed access to the History Tapes. Only some of the very clever students in the red zone school tower were taught History.

We sat by the fire for a while in silence drinking tea. Suddenly, Miss North drew her dressing gown about her knees and said, 'Will you put another log on the fire, please dear?'

I smiled. 'It's a gas fire, Pauline.'

'I'm sorry. My mind wanders sometimes. I was thinking about trees. Is it true there are still trees in the Blue Zone?'

Pauline took something from her dressing gown pocket and put it on the table next to the tea cups.

'What is this?' I asked, picking it up.

'Bark,' she said and seeing me frown added, 'The skin of a tree.'

'Trees had skins? Like people?'

'Oh yes Suzi, trees are just like people. They grow from seeds, they put down roots, they die when their time comes. Some grow straight, some grow crooked.'

She watched as I turned the bark over and over in my hand. Then she leaned across and switched off my tape recorder. 'Would you like a History lesson, Suzi?'

'I'm not . . . '

'Are you afraid to know what really happened in the past?'

'They say it was awful. Best forgotten.'

' "They"? '

'The government. The Video-priests.'

'And what do *you* think?'

I looked round the book-lined room, 'I used to be so sure. But not anymore . . . '

Pauline North showed me to the door of her flat. We shook hands. 'Will you come again, Suzi?'

'Yes, if you'll let me.'

'Come any time. And use the service stairs next time. Goodbye.'

* * *

When I returned to the flat a week later the door was ajar. I knocked and went in. The flat was completely empty, all the books and furniture, everything was gone. My footsteps echoed alarmingly through the empty rooms so I tip-toed about like a criminal.

I was just about to leave when I saw the slither of bark on the floor behind the door. Slipped it into my pocket and ran.

Back at the office I sat down at my computer and asked it for Pauline Lesley North's lifescan. The data disk whirled for a few seconds, then the screen flashed: 'No such citizen'.

Next I asked it for Peter Jones's lifescan. I scribbled down his address and ran from the office, hoping against hope that I would be in time.

What to do

Oral work in pairs or small groups

1 Why did Suzi want to meet Pauline North?

2 Why did Peter Jones react the way he did when Suzi first spoke to him?

3 Why was Pauline North reluctant to meet with Suzi?

4 Why did the books make Suzi feel uneasy?

5 Why did Pauline ask Suzi if her tape recorder told 'the truth'?

6 Suzi said Pauline had been born 'in the old way'. What do you think Suzi meant by that?

7 What do you think the 'Brain Laser' is used for?

8 What did Suzi think when the screen flashed 'No such citizen'?

9 What do you think Suzi found when she got to Peter Jones's address?

10 Why were the army guarding the reservoir? What else in the story gives you a clue about how life in the future might be different from life today?

Writing

1 You are a friend of Suzi Hayman. You work in the same office. She disappears and no one seems to know where or why. You open her desk and discover a notebook and some tapes.
Write a story about how these tapes and the notebook help you find Suzi.

2 You are a reporter with Video News. You were sent to report on The Water War. There are some clues about this war in the story.
Write a report on this war. Describe who it was between, why it started and how it was won.
You will have to invent names, dates and places. You might include a map to show which events happened, when and where.

3 Imagine you are living in the year 2992. The government controls all newspapers, TV and radio. It also controls all schools. There are no such things as books.
It is forbidden to talk or write about the past.
One day you find something that makes you curious about the past. You decide to try to find out more about your own history, and your parents and grandparents.
Describe the thing that you found, where you found it, why it made you want to know more.
Next describe how you discovered more about your family's history. What did you discover? How did you feel about what you uncovered?
Remember that your research was illegal. You might be afraid as you write about it.

Secrets

Anna stood in the darkness, perfectly still, waiting. Far below the music stopped. There was a roll of drums and the ring master cried, 'And now, ladies and gentlemen, girls and boys, we are proud to present the Queen of the High Wire, Anna Bonnati!'

A single brilliant spotlight fell on Anna, and cast her giant shadow across the roof of the circus tent. As Anna stepped off the tiny platform on to the wire the light caught the sequins on her cape. These tiny points of light, like stars, spread across the canvas cave of the big top. Anna felt as if she could do anything. She felt powerful, free. She felt as if she could have walked across the void without a wire.

Up there, wrapped in applause, focusing all her energies on one step, then another, then another . . . she could forget about Perry. Forget his sullen moods, his drinking, his gambling.

Half an hour later Anna was back in the real world. The show was over. The audience had gone. The circus tent was littered with crumpled sweet wrappers and empty cans. The night crew were gathering in the ring. They were the circus hands who swept up, cleaned the toilets, raked over the sawdust, fed the animals and mucked them out, checked the lights, the sound systems, the trapeze rigging and a thousand other routine jobs.

Anna stood in the shadows under the bandstand. She was waiting for a young man called Kurt. Kurt Ashby was one of the night crew. He was in love with Anna and wanted to marry her. But Anna was already married, to Perry.

They'd been married for ten years. At first they had been very happy together, but just recently they did nothing but row. Anna had asked him for a divorce, but he refused.

Perry would get drunk and taunt Anna, 'Queen of the High Wire! Think you're it, don't you? With your nose in the air, and your name in lights! Your Majesty, take care not to trip. The higher you fly, the harder you fall.'

Perry was a clown. He did a double act with another clown

called Sobbo. Perry wore a huge monkey suit, that made him look like King Kong. Perry had spent hours watching real gorillas. He could eat, walk, talk, even scratch himself like a gorilla. Perry looked so like a real gorilla that children and adults were sometimes scared when he jumped out of the ring into the audience. So when Sobbo caught him in his butterfly net Perry would take off his furry head-piece to let the audience into the secret.

Kurt walked slowly over to the bandstand. Anna touched his arm gently. She didn't look at him, but whispered, 'Midnight. The same place. He's playing poker.'

* * *

Anna was alone. Perry was playing cards with the circus manager and some of the other clowns in the bar. He'd play until five or six o'clock in the morning. She slipped out of the caravan and made her way to the props store. This was the big shed where all the equipment needed for the show was stored. It was always kept locked. But Anna had managed to get a key.

Kurt rapped gently on the window and Anna let him in. The storeroom was in darkness. They sat down on some bales of straw. Kurt put his arms around her and said, 'Tomorrow.'

Anna shivered. 'But if it goes wrong . . . if you're caught . . .?'

'I won't be caught. I'm going to spend the rest of my life married to you, not in jail. I'll be careful.'

'All right, but go through it one more time. Tell me, now, exactly what you're going to do . . . '

Kurt kissed her. 'It'll work. As long as we're careful.'

But they hadn't been careful enough. Perry knew all about Kurt's midnight meetings with Anna. He was there now, watching and listening to every word that was said. Inside the monkey suit that lay in a heap, in the dark, in the far corner of the dusty storeroom. So near.

The following day Kurt slipped a note under the door of Perry's dressing room. Perry found it a couple hours later when he went to put on his make-up. It said:

'I know something about your wife that you should know. Meet me tonight, after the show, at midnight. Block B. Come alone. A friend.'

Perry smiled when he read the note. He folded it carefully and slipped it into his pocket.

* * *

That night Anna did her act as usual. But for once the stars didn't dance in the heavens. She felt small and alone, as if the big top was empty, as if she had arrived late and the audience, sick of waiting, had left. The wire felt as sharp as a blade beneath her feet. Midway between the safety of the two platforms she stopped. Held in the spotlight, thinking about Kurt and Perry, she froze. Just for a second. Then she made up her mind and walked on.

Block B was the section of the circus, backstage, where all the performing animals were kept. Kurt spent much of his time in Block B. He was particularly friendly with Bonzo, a huge ancient gorilla. He gave him an apple every night when he cleaned out his cage.

Kurt's plan was simple. He was going to strangle Perry and dump him in Bonzo's cage. Perry used to spend a lot of time with Bonzo, watching him. Everyone knew that Bonzo was getting rather grumpy in his old age. They'd all jump to the same conclusion.

Kurt went to Block B just before midnight. It was deserted and in darkness, as usual. Kurt walked over to Bonzo's cage and looked in. For a second, in the gloom he thought he saw two gorillas in the cage. Then two strong, hairy hands shot through the bars and took him by the throat. Kurt, letting go of life, gave a long, rattling gasp, like a camel snuffling in its sleep.

The coroner's verdict was 'Death by misadventure'. Bonzo would have to be killed.

Perry went to see the gorilla for the last time. Tomorrow the vet would come and destroy him. Perry stared into the beast's deep, brown eyes and shuddered. 'You know all my secrets, don't you, Bonzo?' Perry slipped an apple between the bars and walked away.

What to do

Oral work in pairs or small groups

1 Why did Anna feel she could have 'walked across the void without a wire'?

2 Why do you think Perry refused to divorce Anna?

3 What was Anna thinking when she stopped for a moment 'midway between the safety of the two platforms'?

4 Why did Kurt think he would get away with the murder?

5 How might Perry's plan have gone wrong?

6 Anna knew all about Kurt's plan. How do you think she reacted when she heard Kurt was dead?

7 Do you think Perry told Anna how Kurt had died?

Writing

1 You are a police inspector. Two months after Kurt's death you receive an anonymous note:

> 'When is a gorilla not a gorilla?'
> Kurt Ashby's death wasn't an accident.'

You are puzzled by this note and decide to investigate. Make a list of all the people you would question, together with the questions you might ask them.
Use this list to help you to write a description of how you found out the truth about Kurt's death.